SCOOBY-DOO!

Case Files #2:

The Summer Camp Cyclops

Written by James Gelsey

A
LITTLE APPLE
PAPERBACK

SCHOLASTIC INC.

New York Toronto London Auckland Sydney
Mexico City New Delhi Hong Kong Buenos Aires

No part of this publication may be reproduced in whole or in part, or stored in a retrieval system, or transmitted in any form or by any means, electronic, mechanical, photocopying, recording, or otherwise, without written permission of the publisher. For information regarding permission, write to Scholastic Inc., Attention: Permissions Department, 557 Broadway, New York, NY 10012.

ISBN-10: 0-439-91592-9

ISBN-13: 978-0-439-91592-2

Copyright © 2007 Hanna-Barbera.

SCOOBY-DOO and all related characters and elements are trademarks of and © Hanna-Barbera.

Published by Scholastic Inc. All rights reserved.

SCHOLASTIC, LITTLE APPLE, and associated logos are trademarks and/or registered trademarks of Scholastic Inc.

Designed by Michael Massen

12 11 10 9 8 7 6 5 4 3 2   7 8 9 10 11/0

Special thanks to Duendes del Sur for cover and interior illustrations.

Printed in the U.S.A.

First printing, June 2007

Hi! I'm Velma Dinkley, and this is Daphne, Fred, Shaggy, and of course, Scooby-Doo! We're the gang from Mystery, Inc. and we're really glad you could join us. We've just come back from a super-tough case that we think you may be really interested in.

In these pages, we've recorded everything that happened at the scene of the mystery. You'll

find notes, photographs, and even puzzles to help you identify the suspects and connect the clues. When you're done, you'll be on your way to figuring out who's behind the Mystery of the Summer Camp Cyclops!

So sharpen your pencil, get out your magnifying glass, and turn the page for your first Case Files entry. Good luck!

From the desk of
Mystery, Inc.

It was a beautiful summer day, and the Mystery Machine was cruising along the twisting mountain roads.

"Like, what's with the long and winding road, Fred?" Shaggy asked from the back of the Mystery Machine.

"That's the way they build these mountain roads," Fred answered. "Having serpentine roads like these makes it a lot easier to go up the mountain."

"It also makes it a lot easier to get van-sick," Shaggy said.

"We should be there pretty soon," I said as I checked the map on my lap.

We were on our way to Camp Sakasnaks. Fred went there when he was seven and eight years old. The new camp director, Joe Pfeffer, had invited us to investigate some strange things that had been going on up there. But we didn't want to tell Shaggy and Scooby, otherwise they never would have gotten into the van.

Little Freddie Jones

Camp Sakasnaks

back in the day.

"Tell me again why we're going?" Shaggy asked. "And more importantly—"

"Rhat's for runch!" Scooby added.

"You, like, took the words right out of my mouth, Scoob," Shaggy said.

"Yeah, but too bad you can't eat them," Daphne said with a smile. "Then you'd never go hungry!"

Fred told Shaggy and Scooby that Uncle Joe invited us up to referee the annual Saka-snaks Showdown. That was what they called their mini-Olympics for the counselors. Fred said they did it every summer on the day before the campers arrived.

"I didn't know you had an Uncle Joe," Shaggy said.

"He's not my real uncle," Fred chuckled. "He's the camp director. And when I was a camper, he was just my bunk counselor. But even then, he wanted everyone to call him Uncle Joe. And you know what else? Back then he used to dream about one day owning the camp. I guess his dream came true."

He may have gotten his dream, but it seemed to me like it was becoming more and more of a nightmare. After all, Uncle Joe had been getting threatening letters, and all kinds of crazy things had been happening at camp.

It was a good thing the campers weren't there yet.

Just then, Daphne's cell phone rang. She reached into her handbag and looked at the number that was calling.

"Hmm, I don't recognize this number," she said.

"Let me see," Fred said. She showed him the phone and Fred nodded.

"That's the camp's number," Fred explained. "I gave Uncle Joe your cell phone number in case he needed to reach us. I hope that's okay."

"Sure, Fred," Daphne said. She flipped open the phone and spoke to Uncle Joe. He seemed curious about how close we were to camp. Daphne told him, nodded, and then closed the phone. She looked out the windshield with a concerned expression on her face.

"What's up, Daphne?" Fred asked.

"Uncle Joe said to keep our eyes peeled for anything suspicious as we drive into camp," she said.

That word caught my attention.

"Suspicious?" I asked. "What did he mean?"

"He didn't say," Daphne answered.

"Well, I don't see anything–whoa!" Fred gasped.

Yikes!

A giant banner hung over the entrance to the camp's driveway. Its big, bold, blue letters spelled out, "Greetings, campers." But black spray paint covered most of the first word, changing the sign to read, "Go home, campers."

Fred slowed the van as he turned into the driveway and stopped beneath the banner.

"I guess that would count as suspicious," Daphne said.

"I have a hunch we may be in for more than we originally bargained for," I said.

That banner had us all a little freaked out about what we'd find on the other side of the camp gates. But before you read all about it, take some time to sharpen your detective skills with the puzzle on the next page.

Puzzle #1

Fill in the crossword puzzle. The clues are all about summer camp. When you're done, unscramble the shaded letters to answer the bonus question on the next page.

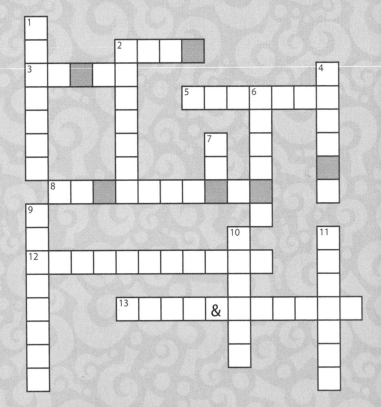

ACROSS

2. A body of water surrounded by land; "Go jump in a _____"
3. A long boat, paddles make it go
5. The counselor blows on this to get your attention
8. Use this to see in the dark
12. The main ingredient of s'mores
13. Lanyard making, pottery and tie-dye are all part of this activity

DOWN

1. The sport that involves a bow and arrows
2. You get these when the mail comes
4. A game played on a court with rackets
6. When it's too hot to wear pants, you can wear these
7. _____ repellent
9. Sit around this to sing songs and roast hotdogs
10. Wear this in the rain to keep dry
11. This keeps your water cool, and you can drink from it too

BONUS QUESTION:

What's Scooby-Doo's favorite summer camp activity?

— — — — — —

(Of course!)

How'd you do? Feeling good about your detective skills now? Great! Read on so you can see what happened when we rolled down the driveway and began our unforgettable visit to Camp Sakasnaks!

From the desk of
Mystery, Inc.

The Mystery Machine rumbled down the gravel driveway from the main road into camp. As we pulled in, the road curved to the right, giving us a view of the lake in the center of camp.

"There she is," Fred announced. "Lake Baxter and Camp Sakasnaks!"

Fred stopped the van next to a golf cart in front of a low log cabin. A red and yellow "Office" sign hung on the cabin's door. As we got out of the van, the office door swung open and two people stepped out, a man and a woman dressed exactly alike.

They were both wearing red and yellow collared camp shirts and tan shorts. The tall, skinny man also had a pair of sunglasses perched on top of his head and a pair of reading glasses dangling from a string around his neck.

"Fred!" the man shouted. "Glad to see ya! Glad to see ya! You look great! Haven't changed a bit!"

Uncle Joe,
the camp director

Fred shook the man's hand.

"Thanks, Uncle Joe, you look great too," he said. "And these are my friends." Fred introduced the rest of us.

"Thanks for having us up here, Mr. Pfeffer," Daphne said.

"Please, call me Uncle Joe," he said. "Call me Uncle Joe. Everyone in camp calls me Uncle Joe, right Mindy?"

The woman next to Uncle Joe smiled and nodded.

"That's right," she said. "I'm Mindy Morgan, the arts and crafts counselor." Then she turned to Uncle Joe. "You told me you were going to call the supply house. If the rest of the supplies don't get here before the campers, it'll be your fault, Uncle Joe!"

"I'm sorry, Mindy, but I've been swamped, just swamped," Uncle Joe said. "I'll get to it right after lunch."

Mindy Morgan shook her head. "That's what you always say, Uncle Joe," she said. "You mark my words: One of these days you'll take me seriously!" With that, she turned and stormed off.

"Jeez, Uncle Joe," Daphne said. "She seemed really upset!"

Mindy Morgan,

the arts & crafts
counselor

"Never you mind her, kids, she's always carrying on about something or other. Freddy, my boy, you're all grown up, all grown up!"

Fred looked out over the lake and smiled.

"Sure brings back memories," he said. "Everything looks as great as ever!"

"Glad to hear it! Glad to hear it!" Uncle Joe said. "How was the trip? No problems? Any problems?"

I overheard Shaggy whisper to Scooby-Doo, "Like, is it him, or am I hearing double?"

Scooby snickered, "Reeheeheeheehee."

"I'd love to show everyone around before lunch and the Sakasnaks Showdown," Fred said.

"Plenty of time for tours! Plenty of time!" Uncle Joe said. "But first, did you, um... see anything suspicious on your way in?"

"Just the welcome banner," I said.

Uncle Joe's eyes widened in horror. "No! Not the banner too!" he cried. He grabbed a walkie-talkie from his waist.

"Mr. Grady? Mr. Grady?" Uncle Joe said. "Check the welcome banner. Over." Uncle Joe held the walkie-talkie to his ear waiting for a response. "Uncle Joe to Mr. Grady. Uncle Joe to Mr. Grady. Do you read me? Over."

"Over!" Mr. Grady replied.

Uncle Joe jumped about two feet into the air. Standing directly behind him was an older man wearing faded overalls and a checkered work shirt. A wide-brimmed hat shaded his scraggly face.

"Please don't do that, Mr. Grady," Uncle Joe said. Uncle Joe introduced us to Mr. Grady, the camp caretaker. Then he told Mr. Grady about the banner.

"And I suppose you want me to shimmy up there, take the thing down, clean it up, and put it back before the end of the day," Mr. Grady said.

Uncle Joe nodded. "You see, that's why I need you here, Mr. Grady. You're one of the only people here who really understands camp. Now I gotta run and take care of a couple of things before lunch. Fred, you and your friends should make yourself at home and look around. Know what I mean? Know what I mean? I'll see you at lunch."

Uncle Joe went back into the office, leaving Mr. Grady with us. His right eye squinted shut as he looked us over. When he got to Fred, he stopped.

"You look familiar," Mr. Grady said.

"That's because I was a camper here," Fred said. "It was a while back."

Entry #2

Mr. Grady,

the
camp caretaker

"Sonny, the years may blur together, but the faces never do," Mr. Grady said. "I've been here so long I can walk this entire place in my sleep. I've got the keys to every darn building in this camp!" Mr. Grady took out a huge key ring and shook it violently so that all the keys jingled. "Not only that," he continued, "to help that Pfeffer kid I even engraved little pictures on the keys so he'd know where they go, like this one here." Mr. Grady held up the key to the boathouse — it had a little canoe engraved on it. But do you think that Pfeffer kid has ever paid me a decent wage? No sirree. All I got to show for all my years of hard work is one of these things."

Mr. Grady took a shiny red pin from his shirt pocket. Its big yellow letters read, "ASK ME."

"A few of us gotta wear these stupid things cause we've been here the longest," Mr. Grady grumbled. "All I can say is that I can't buy a single grocery with a pin that says ASK ME!"

Mr. Grady huffed off, leaving us alone in front of the office.

"I remember being creeped out by him when I was a kid," Fred said. "Around the campfires they used to tell stories about his old shack in the woods where he kept a monster chained up that used to eat the bad campers."

That was all Shaggy and Scooby-Doo needed to hear.

"Sounds like a great camp, Fred," Shaggy said. "But me and Scooby have somewhere else to be right now."

"Where?" asked Daphne.

"Anywhere that's not here!" Shaggy replied.

Someone we just met made quite an impression on us. So if you can work your way through the next puzzle, you'll understand who we're talking about and why we think that person is important to remember.

Puzzle #2

The words in the list below are hidden in this puzzle. Find them and circle them. Then unscramble the leftover letters to spell out the name of the second suspect.

ARCHERY	BUGS	FRIENDS	SWIMMING
BATIK	CAMPER	FUN	STABLE
BASEBALL	CAMPFIRE	LAKE	TENNIS
BASKETBALL	COLOR WAR	NATURE	TENT
BOATING	COUNSELORS	SMORES	
BUNKS	DIVE	SUN	

```
m   r       l   d i v e     b
    a   e k a l     a     a e
    w   r       a       s r
    r s i n n e t   k i   d
s r o l e s n u o c e f f
    l y t e n t   t p s   u
f   o     s g u b m     a   n
a r c h e r y a a b       b
e   i     c l c s o s u n   b
  r   e a l     e a     a s
    u m n   g   r t     t k t
    p t   d     o   i n   a
  e     a   s   m n k u     b
r       n     s g b       l
    s w i m m i n g     r   e
```

The suspect's name is: __ __ __ __ __ __ __

We could see how a little kid could be scared of Mr. Grady. But we knew that Fred loved camp, so there must have been all kinds of other great stuff happening there. So read on and follow us on a tour of Camp Sakasnaks.

From the desk of
Mystery, Inc.

"Come on, gang, let me show you around," Fred said.

From the office, Fred led us into the heart of camp. There was a giant campfire circle right in the middle. Four rings of wooden benches surrounded the pit where some charred old logs sat. Old wooden buildings formed a semi-circle behind one side of the pit. Each had a sign announcing what the building was for.

"Over there's the arts and crafts shack," Fred said. He pointed to the tie-dye paint-ed building in the middle of the row. "Next to it is the radio station. And on the other side's the nature center."

"It seems to me like the whole camp is a

nature center," Daphne said as she swatted away a mosquito.

"This is where we used to have the campfires," Fred said.

"You mean the creepy campfires where they frighten young children with stories about monsters locked in sheds?" Shaggy asked.

"That, and have s'mores!" Fred added.

"S'mores? I ruv s'mores!" Scooby barked happily.

I strolled around to the far side of the campfire circle and found two other paths.

"Where do these go, Fred?" I asked.

"One of them goes towards the sports fields and the boys' bunks," Fred said. "The other goes down to the waterfront."

"You mean the lakefront," a woman said coming out of the arts and crafts shack. She was pretty tall and wore a pair of black sweat pants over her red one-piece bathing suit. She was tying up a purple lanyard string with her whistle on it.

"Around here, we like to call it the lakefront," she repeated. "I'm Harriet Boyle, Lakefront Director. You kids new on staff? Then you'd better follow me down to the

Harriet Boyle,
lakefront director

lake for your swim tests. No one goes into my lake without a swim test."

She started walking down the path to the lake before any of us could explain who we were. So we followed her anyway. And that's when Daphne noticed something stuck to Harriet's black sweat pants.

"Hey, isn't that one of those ASK ME pins?" Daphne whispered to me.

I saw it and nodded. "I guess she's been here a long time too."

"She must have started after I left," Fred said. "Because I don't remember her."

The path opened up onto a narrow strip of beach by the lake. To one side stood a yellow boathouse. A yellow dock reached from the beach out into the lake. Two counselors were sunning themselves on the wooden dock.

"Hey! Get off that dock!" Harriet yelled. "No one gave you permission to be out there!"

The two counselors jumped up and ran off the dock.

"What's the big idea, Harriet?" one of them said as he ran by her. "We were just getting some sun."

"Get your sun someplace else before I report you to Uncle Joe," Harriet replied.

"You're as bad as Uncle Joe," the other counselor said. "He's so strict about the rules, this place is no fun anymore!"

The counselors took off as Harriet walked over to the boathouse and locked the door with a key she had taken from her pocket. I noticed that the key was large and old-fashioned looking. There was a canoe and a paddle engraved on it. We walked over to

Harriet Boyle runs a tight ship!

Entry #2

where she was standing, and noticed a green tent pitched behind the boathouse. Harriet saw us staring at the tent. She got upset, walked over, and lowered the flaps over the tent's window screens.

"You know, the camp just built a brand-new air-conditioned bunkhouse," she said. "And that's where I was supposed to live this summer. But then Uncle Shmoe — I mean, Joe — told me I had to sleep here, for safety and security reasons."

"When I was a camper here, the waterfront director always slept by the boathouse," Fred said.

"I told you, it's called the lakefront," Harriet said. "And I'm the Lakefront Director. And I do not sleep in tents!"

"She may not sleep in tents, but man, she sure sounds intense!" Shaggy said to Scooby-Doo.

Harriet walked over to Shaggy and Scooby and asked which one wanted to go first for their swim test. Shaggy and Scooby each pointed to the other.

"A couple of wiseguys, huh," she said. "Then how about a double dip?" Harriet picked them up and carried one under each arm along the yellow dock that reached out over the lake.

"You look like you can handle the dog paddle," she said to Scooby. But just before she could throw either of them in, the rest of us ran after her.

"Hold on!" Fred called. "We're not counselors here or anything. We're just visiting. Uncle Joe invited us up to help out with the Sakasnaks Showdown!"

Harriet put Shaggy and Scooby down.

"Fine," she spat. "I've got better things to do anyway, like cleaning out the canoes. But the next time any of you kids step foot on my lakefront, you're going in!"

Wow! How would you like to take swimming lessons from her?

Solve this next puzzle to find our second suspect.

Puzzle #3

The name of our second suspect is written below, but you'll need to use the Zoinksabet to decode it!

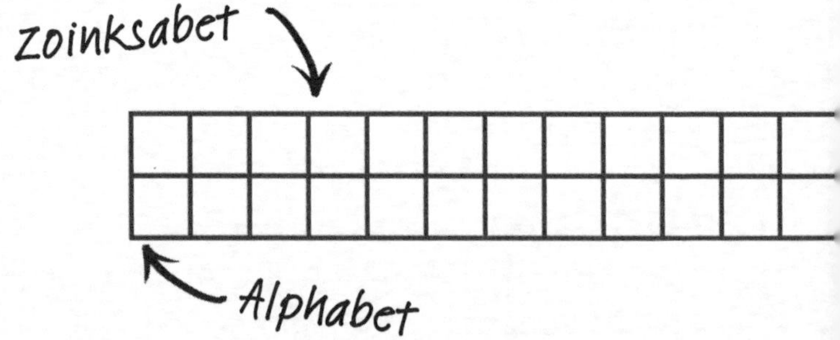

Zoinksabet →

Alphabet ←

Here's a hint: using the Zoinksabet,
Zoinks = Yjcheq

Here's how to make your Zoinksabet decoder:

◎ In the top row of boxes, write the letters Z, O, I, N, K, and S. Then write the rest of the alphabet from A-Z leaving out the letters Z, O, I, N, K, and S. Those letters should appear only once, at the beginning of the Zoinksabet.

◎ In the boxes below the Zoinksabet write the letters of the regular alphabet from A-Z. Remember, when writing both the Zoinksabet and the alphabet, write from left to right, and use only one letter per box.

◎ To crack the code, swap the letter of the Zoinksabet with the letter of the alphabet directly below it.

Zoinksabet

Alphabet

The suspect is: Bzppckr Ojxfk
For extra credit, decode the suspect's motive:
        Qbk bzrkq fcucha ch z rkhr!

Okay, so that makes two pretty interesting people we've met so far at Camp Sakasnaks. But after we visited the lakefront it was time for Shaggy and Scooby's favorite part of the day: lunch! So read on to see what happened when we made our way over to the dining hall.

From the desk of
Mystery, Inc.

As we followed the path away from the lakefront, Scooby-Doo suddenly stopped. His nose shot straight up into the air and twitched.

"What is it, Scoob?" asked Shaggy.

Scooby took a deep breath, stretching open his nostrils as wide as they could go.

"Racaroni and cheese!" Scooby cheered.

Shaggy's head spun around.

"Which way? Where?" Shaggy asked. He looked in all directions for the macaroni and cheese.

"Ris way," Scooby said. His body assumed the pointer position: back flat, his nose pointing forward, his tail straight out behind him. He began walking in slow, measured steps, his nose constantly twitching. Shaggy crept along carefully behind him.

"That's right, Scoob," Shaggy whispered. "Take us to the noodles."

Fred rolled his eyes. "Come on, you two, I know a shortcut to the dining hall." Fred turned and stepped off the path and into the trees.

"Rait for ree!" Scooby barked. He turned and dove into the woods after Fred. Daphne, Shaggy, and I followed. When we came out, we found ourselves behind the camp's large dining hall. There we saw someone dressed all in white hosing out an enormous metal pot. It was large enough for Scooby to climb into . . . which he almost did because he could smell the cheese that was being rinsed out.

"Just in time for lunch, I see," Uncle Joe said as he came up behind us. "And you still know the shortcuts, too."

Fred nodded.

"See you inside," Uncle Joe said. "You can sit at my table."

As Uncle Joe went into the building, we heard the man in white mutter something to himself.

"What was that?" I asked.

"I said, 'Nice. Not even a hello'," the man said. "The camp director walked right by me and didn't even say hello. Talk about adding insult to injury."

"Injury? Did you get hurt?" asked Daphne.

The man shook his head. "No. Well, not physically," he said. "But there's more than one way to hurt someone, you know?"

We didn't know what to say and were about to go inside when the man kept talking.

"My name's Chris Canarsie. I'm the dishwasher," he said.

"Yeah, I thought you looked familiar," Fred said. "I was here as a camper years ago. And I remember you working in the kitchen even back then."

Chris Canarsie nodded. He explained how he'd been working in the kitchen for years doing every job but cooking. But this year the head chef's job opened up. And he really wanted it. He tried to convince Uncle Joe to give it to him, but Uncle Joe brought in someone from outside camp.

"That's too bad," Daphne said.

"Tell me about it," Chris said. "How can someone cook for camp if they've never even been to camp? That Uncle Joe dashed my hopes!

"Ask"
Chris Canarsie

And I told him as much too. He said he'd pay for me to take cooking classes. But why do I need cooking classes? I've been working in the kitchen for years! And you know how he rewarded me for my years of service? He gave me this stupid ASK ME pin to wear!"

A three-chimed bell rang out on the loud-speakers throughout camp.

"Lunch!" Fred announced.

Saved by the bell! We waved goodbye to Chris Canarsie and followed Fred inside. The camp dining room was a large, open space with eight long rows of rectangular picnic tables. Only four of the tables were being used by the camp staff. The rest were going to be filled when the campers arrived the next day. Uncle Joe's table was off to the side.

"Over here, Fred!" he called. We sat down at his table. A woman in a camp shirt was standing beside Uncle Joe.

"This is Nurse Womack," Uncle Joe said. "Best nurse there is, no question. No question about it!"

The nurse didn't look very pleased with the compliment.

"Thank you, Uncle Joe," she said. "Of course, it would be a lot easier to do my job if the health center had a working air conditioner."

Uncle Joe looked embarrassed, but stayed silent.

Nurse Womack continued. "Ours is still broken, and it needs to be working by the time the kids arrive tomorrow, or else there'll be heck to pay!" She stormed off

Entry #4

Nurse Womack. How'd you like her to take your temperature?

before Uncle Joe could reply. He turned his attention to us.

"Now then, Fred, remember how this works?" asked Uncle Joe.

"I think so," Fred answered. "During the summer, every bunk sends a camper into the kitchen to get a cart with the trays of food for the table. But since there aren't any campers here . . . "

And at that moment, Fred and Uncle Joe each touched their index finger to the side of their nose. Daphne and I noticed them right away and did it also. That left Shaggy and Scooby-Doo staring at us with puzzled looks on their faces.

"Do you, like, all suddenly have the same kind of itch on your noses?" asked Shaggy.

Fred smiled.

"No, Shaggy, this is how we choose who has to get the food for the table," Fred replied. "Last one with their finger on their nose loses."

"Tell me, Scoob, have you ever heard such a ridiculous thing before?" Shaggy said. But when he turned to look at his pal, he saw that Scooby was holding his paw against his nose.

"You too, Scooby-Doo?" Shaggy sighed. "Fine, I'll get the food."

Shaggy stood up and went through the kitchen door. When he didn't return after a couple of minutes, the rest of us at the table looked at each other.

"Oh, no!" they cried. "We sent Shaggy to get the food all by himself! What have we done?"

Entry #14

Well, that was a mistake we won't ever make again! And speaking of mistakes, we just met someone who thinks that Uncle Joe has made a big one. Figure out this next puzzle to discover who our third and final suspect is.

Puzzle #4

Circle the one letter that's different in each pair of words. We did the first one for you. Then unscramble those letters to finish the name of our next suspect.

DON(A)TE and TONED

BRACES and SABER

PEARS and PHRASE

PROUDEST and SPOUTED

ENCLOSE and CLONES

PLEASES and ASLEEP

NATION and CONTAIN

WAITER and WRITE

MEANING and ENIGMA

PRECISE and RECIPE

ASTUTE and STATURE

SPOILED and SLOPED

_ _ _ I _   _ _ _ A _ _ _ _

Believe it or not, meeting Chris Canarsie wasn't the most memorable part of our visit to the dining room. Neither was the fact that Shaggy ate a whole table's worth of food all by himself. Read on, and you'll discover what really made that lunch unforgettable.

From the desk of
Mystery, Inc.

While we were eating, Uncle Joe got up and stepped onto a small platform at the front of the dining room. He tapped on a standing microphone a couple of times to make sure it was on.

"Can I have everybody's attention please? Attention please?" he said. "As you know, right after lunch we'll all be heading to the sports fields for our annual Sakasnaks Showdown!"

The camp counselors cheered wildly.

"Settle down, please. Settle down," Uncle Joe said. "And after that, we'll go into our final preparations for the first day of camp tomorrow!"

More cheering filled the dining room, rattling the windows. Uncle Joe gestured for everyone to quiet down again.

"But before all that, let me say how happy I am that all of you are here to help me make this Camp Sakasnak's best summer ever!" he shouted.

Again, everyone cheered and clapped their hands. The whole dining room then erupted into song.

"Hey! That's the Camp Sakasnaks anthem!" Fred said. He stood up, put his hand over his heart, and joined in the singing. None of us could ever remember hearing Fred sing before! But believe it or not, things got even weirder!

Suddenly a loud wail drifted into the dining room, drowning out the singing. As the voices died down, the wailing grew louder and louder until we all had our hands over our ears — even Scooby-Doo! Then something burst through the doors.

It was a giant cyclops! Its massive body barely fit into its torn brown pants and checkered flannel shirt. Its big, bloodshot brown eye searched around the dining room. And when it saw Uncle Joe, the creature sprang into action. It ran over to the platform and grabbed Uncle Joe with one hand, the microphone with the other.

"CAMP'S CLOSED!" it hissed. "And if you ever want to see your Uncle Joe again, make sure it never re-opens!"

And with that, the Cyclops threw down the microphone and ran out of the dining room with Uncle Joe. We were all too stunned to move. That's when one of the counselors jumped up and shouted, "It's true! The myth about the Sakasnaks Cyclops is true! I'm getting out of here!"

The counselor ran out of the dining room, beginning a stampede of staff members.

"This is terrible!" Daphne cried.

"I know," Fred agreed. "With Uncle Joe gone and the entire staff spooked, there's no way camp will be able to open tomorrow."

"Like, aren't you forgetting something else?" Shaggy asked.

"What?" I asked.

"Like, that there's a great big ugly one-eyed giant monster running around?" Shaggy said.

"Shaggy's right," Fred nodded. "We have to capture that Cyclops. And then we'll find

Entry #5

That's one scary Cyclops!

Uncle Joe and get the camp staff calmed down."

Shaggy and Scooby-Doo looked at each other.

"Scoob and I would love to help," Shaggy began. "But you know how we deal with great big ugly one-eyed giant monsters."

"What is it?" asked Daphne.

"That Scooby can tell you in one word," Shaggy said.

"RUN!" Scooby barked. He and Shaggy turned to take off, but I grabbed Scooby's collar and Fred took hold of the back of Shaggy's shirt. Shaggy and Scooby's legs were moving, but their bodies weren't going anywhere.

"Sorry, fellas, but we're all going to have to work together to solve this mystery," I said.

"First, I want to make sure none of the counselors leave camp," Fred said. "I'll go down to the office and make an announcement asking them to stay in their bunks. They can use the time to finish getting set up for the campers."

"I'll go with you, Fred," Daphne said. "That way we can start looking for clues outside the dining room. Maybe we'll find something that tells us which way the Cyclops creature ran."

I decided to look around inside the dining room with Shaggy and Scooby-Doo. We agreed to meet back at the main office. And then we split up to begin our search for clues. I explored the area in the front of the room around the platform and microphone stand. Meanwhile, Shaggy and Scooby glanced around and noticed the other deserted lunch tables.

I overheard Shaggy say, "Man, it's too bad no one got a chance to finish their lunch." I knew where he was going with that. I watched as he counted the plates still piled high with macaroni and cheese. I heard Scooby's stomach grumble and spun around.

"Oh, no you don't," I said. "We've got more important things to do than eat right now."

Shaggy gasped in horror.

"Velma, like how could you say such a thing?" Shaggy asked as he covered Scooby's ears.

"Oh, brother!" I said. I focused my attention back on the ground and something caught my eye. I took a quick photo, so check it out to see if you figure out what I found.

Turn the page for the first clue →

Do you see anything odd in the photo above? Something, maybe, that the Cyclops left behind? Solve the puzzle on the next page to find out if your hunch is correct.

Puzzle #5

All of the vowels and consonants from this message have been jumbled together. But we've left behind V's (for vowels) and C's (for consonants) as placeholders. Take the vowels and consonants from the lists below to re-form the words. Each letter can only be used as many times as it appears on the list. Then re-create the words to reveal the first clue.

C V C   V C C   V V C C V C
_ _ _   _ N _   Y _ _ _ _ _

V C C   C V   C V C
_ _ _   _ _   _ _ _

Vowels
A, A, E, E, E, I, O

Consonants
D, D, L, L, K, M, ~~N~~, N, P, R, S, W, ~~Y~~

You know by now that it takes more than one clue to solve a mystery. So read the next entry to see what else we discovered.

From the desk of
Mystery, Inc.

Shaggy, Scooby, and I left the dining room to meet up with Fred and Daphne down in the main office. But on our way down, the path branched out in two different directions. That's when I realized that we had taken a different path up to the dining room and didn't know which of the two paths led back down to the main office.

"I think the path on the left will take us back to the office," I said.

Shaggy and Scooby thought it was the one on the right.

I didn't want to waste valuable time arguing with them, so I told them to go whichever way they wanted. And with that, I continued down the path on the left. Sure enough, I made it back to the camp office and showed the clue to Fred and Daphne. When I told Fred which path Shaggy and Scooby took, he knew exactly where to find them.

We followed the path that Shaggy and Scooby had taken halfway around the campfire circle, through the woods, and finally emerged by the sports shack, a large covered pavilion. But when we got there, we decided to stay hidden and see what Shaggy and Scooby were up to.

Inside the sports shack were piles of deflated balls. There were basketballs, footballs, kickballs, volleyballs, soccer balls . . . you name it.

"Man, what is this place, some kind of sporting goods graveyard?" Shaggy gulped.

"Raveyard?" Scooby echoed.

"Sorry, pal, poor choice of words," Shaggy said. "Well since we're here, maybe we can help, I'm going to see if there's a pump in the closet over there."

Shaggy went into the closet and found a hand pump.

"Here, Scoob, we'll take turns using this pump," Shaggy said. "You hand me the ball and I'll pump it up."

Scooby gave Shaggy a basketball with the number "12" on it. Shaggy pumped it back up and rolled it away. Scooby then handed Shaggy a football with the number "8" on it. Shaggy pumped that up and rolled it away. Scooby gave Shaggy another basketball.

"Hey, Scooby, this basketball has the same number on it as that first one," Shaggy said. He pumped it up and then started on the next football Scooby gave him.

"This one's just like the first football I did," Shaggy said. He looked over and saw the first football was gone. And so were the two basketballs. "Hey! What's going on here?"

"Ri runno," Scooby shrugged. He looked down next to him and saw the number "12" basketball and number "8" football both deflated!

"Like, how is that possible?" asked Shaggy.

"NO SPORTS! NO CAMP!" an angry voice screeched. Shaggy and Scooby turned around and saw the Cyclops monster standing behind them. It must have taken another path, because we never saw it coming. The Cyclops monster was holding a large nail that it was using to let the air out of the balls as soon as Shaggy inflated them.

"Zoinks!" Shaggy cried.

"Ruh roh!" Scooby exclaimed.

"BOOOOO!" the Cyclops wailed.

Shaggy and Scooby took off screaming out of the pavilion and disappeared into the woods.

"Rich ray, Raggy?" we heard Scooby shout.

"Just follow the path!" Shaggy answered. What he didn't know was that the path they chose made a big circle around the pavilion.

Before Shaggy and Scooby knew it, they were right back where they started — with the Cyclops!

"You'll never escape from the SAKASNAKS CYCLOPS!" the monster shrieked. "HAHAHAHA-HAHAHA!"

The Cyclops ran right toward them. Shaggy and Scooby dove out of the way and watched the creature disappear into the woods. That's when Fred, Daphne, and I ran over to them.

"Are you two all right?" asked Daphne.

"Man, that crazy camp creature almost de-flated me and Scoob just like it did those balls over there!" Shaggy panted.

"It's a good thing Velma told us which path you took," Fred said. "Otherwise we may never have found you."

"Or this," I said. I found something on the ground next to one of the punctured basketballs. Fred and Daphne examined it up close. They noticed some unusual engravings on it. Here's a photo of what we saw:

I found this →

on the floor of
the sports shack.

So do you.think you know what we found? Figure out this next puzzle to make sure you understand what the next clue is.

Puzzle #6

To get the information you'll need from this puzzle, first unscramble the words above the boxes on the next page. Then take the circled letters and unscramble those. All of the words on the list have something to do with camp. Have fun!

UEHUKSONB

SRTA DAN CARSTF

GIECONNA

SOPSRT

NWMIGISM

LEAK

PIALNGY

Solution:

_ _ _ _ _ _ _ _ _   _ _ _

After finding the key to the boathouse, we were beginning to understand who could be behind this mystery. Check out what else we discovered about th Cyclops.

From the desk of
Mystery, Inc.

Once Shaggy and Scooby recovered from their encounter with the Cyclops, we headed back to the campfire circle in the center of camp with our two clues.

"So what's our next step?" Daphne asked.

"I think we should try to figure out places where the Cyclops could have brought Uncle Joe," I suggested.

"But that could be anywhere," Daphne said.

"Not really," Fred said. "We can rule out the bunkhouses right away because the counselors are inside them."

"And we can rule out the sports pavilion, because we were all just there," I added.

But before we could think about any other

places in camp, we heard a scream come from inside the arts and crafts shack. We immediately ran inside to see what was going on. We saw Mindy, the arts and crafts counselor, standing over a row of paint tubs.

"This is awful," she moaned. "And a terrible waste!"

"What's the matter?" asked Fred.

She showed us a row of open paint cans. All of the colors had been swirled together and mixed up. The paints were ruined!

"Who would do something like this?" asked Daphne.

"Sounds like our friendly neighborhood Cyclops was in here," I said.

"Ryclops? Where?" Scooby gasped as he dove under one of the tables.

Daphne shook her head and assured Scooby that the Cyclops wasn't there anymore. It must have snuck into the arts and crafts shack when Mindy and everyone else was at lunch.

"If someone doesn't do something about that monster soon, there's no way we'll be able to start camp tomorrow," Mindy said.

Something suddenly occurred to me, so I

asked Mindy if there was another door to the arts and crafts shack. She said there was a back door that led to a yard that she used for cleaning paintbrushes and hanging things out to dry. Fred and Daphne left to look for clues outside the arts and crafts shack. I told Shaggy and Scooby to follow me, and stepped out the back door into the yard. "You can come out now, Scooby-Doo," I heard Shaggy say. "Fred, Daphne, and Velma just left." Scooby crawled out from beneath the table.

"Before you go, can you two strong fellas help me take these tubs of paint out back?" Mindy asked.

"Strong fellas?" Shaggy repeated. "You mean, like, us?"

I stepped back into the shack. Mindy smiled and nodded. She walked over and picked up one of the tubs with one hand.

"Rou bet!" Scooby agreed. He ran over and grabbed one of the handles. He gave a mighty lift and found himself pulled back down by the weight of the tub.

"They're a little heavy, but I know you strapping guys can handle it," Mindy said to encourage them.

Scooby tried again with two hands and was

Always ready to lend a hand... ... or paw!

barely able to lift the tub off the ground. He struggled with the tub, splashing little blobs of orange paint as he followed Mindy.

"Like, hold up!" Shaggy called. "You're not leaving me alone in this creepy arts shack!" He ran over and grabbed a tub.

They went through the arts shack's storage room to the back door. When they stepped outside, Scooby dropped the tub. Shaggy put down his tub of paint too. Scooby and Shaggy stood there with their arms dangling at their sides.

"Man, I don't know about you, Scooby-Doo,"

Shaggy began, "but my arms are feeling a lot like spaghetti."

Just then Fred and Daphne came running up to us. They had found something!

Do you recognize it? Solve the puzzle on the next page to find out what it is.

Puzzle #7

Place the words below into the grid making sure not to leave any empty spaces. When you're done, unscramble the letters in the shaded squares to spell out the last clue.

CAMP	TRAILS	SINGING	COUNSELORS
TENTS	HIKING	BUG JUICE	RELAY RACES
TRIPS	BUNK BED	COLOR WAR	

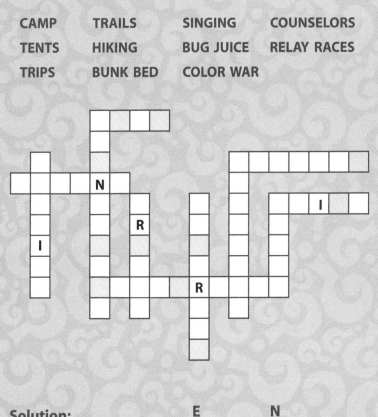

Solution: _ _ _ _ _ E _ _ N _ _ _ _ _

Good detectives take their time to consider all of the information in a case file. So while you think about the suspects and clues we've found, check out how we planned to catch that sneaky Cyclops to save Uncle Joe and Camp Sakasnaks.

From the desk of
Mystery, Inc.

Daphne showed Mindy the lanyard that she and Fred found. "That's odd," Mindy said. We asked her what was odd about it.

"Well, the art supply company hasn't sent me any lanyard gimp yet. That's one of the things that Uncle Joe was supposed to call the supply house about."

"Then where could this have come from?" Daphne wondered.

"Someone who had brought it with them to camp this summer," I said.

"Great thinking, Velma," Fred said. "I think that's the last piece of information we'll need to help us solve this mystery."

And with that, we thanked Mindy and went back to the office to figure out our next step.

Outside the main office, Fred told us that he thought he knew where the Cyclops was hiding Uncle Joe. "I'll go look for him," Fred said, "which means it's up to the rest of you to capture the Cyclops creature."

"No problem, Fred," I said. "I've even been working on a plan. Since we want the Cyclops to think that camp is going to open on schedule, we have to act like everything is back to normal."

Daphne nodded. "That means we should still have the Sakasnaks Showdown!"

"Actually, we only want the Cyclops to believe we're having the Sakasnaks Showdown," I clarified. "So this is how it'll work."

I explained everyone's job. Before going to find Uncle Joe, Fred and Daphne would tell all the counselors to go down to the fields when we called them over the camp's P.A. system. Once there, they would be cheering on the two participants in the showdown.

"But if all of the counselors are cheering," Shaggy asked, "then, like, who's going to be participating?"

And that's when Fred, Daphne, and I looked at Shaggy and Scooby and smiled.

"Oh, no," Shaggy protested. "You know how me and sports don't get along."

"Nothing too it, Shaggy," I said, trying to sound encouraging. "I'm just going to set up a simple obstacle course."

"Don't you mean 'Cyclopstacle' course?" Shaggy asked.

"Ryclops?" Scooby whined. "Ruh oh!"

"Will you do it for . . . a Scooby snack?" asked Daphne.

At the mention of the words "Scooby snack," Scooby's tummy growled loudly. Remembering how he hadn't finished lunch, Scooby was eager for a treat, even if it meant helping to catch a monster.

"Rokay!" he cheered. Daphne tossed the treat into the air and Scooby gobbled it up.

"Once the Cyclops shows up and follows you two through the course," I continued to explain, "Daphne and I will be waiting at the end. The finish line is going to be the tug-of-war rope. We'll get a few counselors to hold each end. When you two reach it, move out of the way. That way, when the Cyclops hits it, we'll wrap him up in it so he can't get away."

"Sounds like a great plan, Velma," Fred

said. "But we don't have much time, so let's get started."

Fred and Daphne went to the bunkhouses. I took Shaggy and Scooby to the sports field to set up the obstacle course. When Daphne returned, she was wearing a red and yellow Camp Sakasnaks shirt. She held three others in her hand, telling us that the counselors thought the showdown would look more realistic if we all wore them. Daphne then ran to the main office to make the announcement over the camp's P.A. system, calling the counselors to the games. After we heard Daphne's voice echo through the trees, I knew it was almost time.

"Okay, fellas, this is it," I said to Shaggy and Scooby-Doo. "Remember to do the whole race and get the Cyclops to follow you to the finish line. Once you get there, move out of the way. Now go on over to the starting line. When I give you the signal, start the race."

Shaggy and Scooby walked across to the far side of the field.

"Okay, Scooby-Doo, no sense in wearing ourselves out," Shaggy said. "Let's just take the race nice and easy."

"Reah, rice and easy," Scooby agreed.

On your mark,
get set . . .

They stood at the starting line, pretending to stretch and warm up. As they did, the counselors trickled onto the field. A few of them stood at the finish line, holding the rope. Once everyone was there, I got ready to start the race. I raised my arm.

"On your mark . . . get set . . . " I said.

"GO!" shouted Uncle Joe. He ran onto the field with Fred as the counselors burst into cheers.

"Hey, look, Fred found Uncle Joe!" Shaggy said.

"Go, fellas!" I shouted.

"Sorry, Velma, we forgot!" Shaggy called back. "Ready, Scooby? On your mark, get set — "

But Scooby had already taken off.

"Hey, that's cheating!" Shaggy called. "Why'd you do that?"

"Ryclops!" Scooby called back.

"Ryclops?" Shaggy said. He turned and saw the Cyclops monster right behind him. "Zoinks! CYCLOPS!" Shaggy took off with the monster in pursuit.

Shaggy quickly caught up to Scooby. They ran through the tires, combat-crawled beneath the benches, jumped through the hula-hoops, zig-zagged through the cones, and leapt over the hurdles, all with the Cyclops hot on their heels. As they approached the finish line, Scooby remembered to duck out of the way. But Shaggy's shoelace came untied at the last minute. He tripped and fell against the finish line rope. The counselors felt the tug and thought it was the Cyclops. They ran around Shaggy over and over, wrapping poor Shaggy up like a mummy.

The Cyclops meanwhile avoided the finish line entirely and kept chasing Scooby. Scooby neared the paths that led into the woods. One path went to the left, and one went to the right. The path on the left circled back around the sports pavilion. The path to the right led back to the center of camp.

"Take the path to the left!" Uncle Joe called. "Left! Left!"

"Reft?" Scooby called back.

"Right!" Uncle Joe replied.

So Scooby ran down the path to the right. We ran after them and even though we didn't see everything first hand, we later found out exactly what happened.

Scooby soon found himself back at the campfire circle at the center of camp. He ran around the campfire three times and then saw the only place that looked familiar: The arts and crafts shack. He ran inside and shot through the shack, into the back room, and out the back door, carefully avoiding the tubs of paint he remembered were there.

An instant later, the Cyclops burst through the door. It didn't know about the paint tubs and crashed right into them. When we finally caught up to them, we found Scooby standing over the paint-splattered Cyclops as it tried to wipe the paint from its eye.

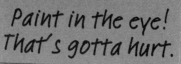

Paint in the eye!
That's gotta hurt.

That was some chase, wasn't it? Uncle Joe has agreed to stand guard over the Cyclops while you get the chance to put all of your hard work to the test. On the next page we'll show you how to organize your crime scene information so we can figure out who's behind this mystery. Good luck!

Solve the Mystery

Take the solutions from each of the puzzles and write them in the chart on the next page according to the instructions:

Entry #8

SUSPECTS Write the name of the suspect from each of the puzzles:	CLUES Write the clue from each of the puzzles:		
	Puzzle #5 Solution: _____	Puzzle #6 Solution: _____	Puzzle #7 Solution: _____
Puzzle #2 Solution: _____			
Puzzle #3 Solution: _____			
Puzzle #4 Solution: _____			

◎ Put an X in the suspect's clue box if he or she can be connected to that clue.

◎ When you're done, there should be only one suspect with an X in each of his or her clue boxes.

◎ Write that person's name here: _____

When you think you know who's behind the mystery, turn the page to see what happened when Uncle Joe unmasked the Sakasnaks Cyclops!

From the desk of
Mystery, Inc.

We all gathered around the Technicolor Cyclops monster. It sat there wiping the paint off its clothes.

"That's what you get for messing with my art supplies," Mindy said.

The rest of the counselors soon arrived to see what was going on. They gawked, pointed, and snickered at the poor Cyclops.

"Thanks for your help, Mr. Grady," Fred said as the caretaker walked over too.

"How did he help?" asked Daphne.

"While you both were setting up the trap, I went to find Mr. Grady so he could take me to that wooden shack of his in the woods," Fred explained. "That's where I guessed the Cyclops was hiding Uncle Joe."

"Fred and Mr. Grady came just in time," Uncle Joe said. "I was beginning to give up hope."

"Well, now's your chance to see who's been behind all this mischief," Daphne said.

Uncle Joe reached over and tugged on the Cyclops's head.

Mystery, Inc. gets their... woman!

"Ouch!" came a woman's voice from inside the mask. "You have to unfasten it in the back first. Like this." The Cyclops reached behind its head and unclipped something. Then it lifted off its head.

"Harriet Boyle!" gasped Uncle Joe. "You?"

"Just as we suspected," Fred said.

"You knew it was her?" Uncle Joe asked.

"How could you possibly have known that?"

"Great question, Uncle Joe," Fred said. "Allow us to explain. When we first got here, we met a few people who all seemed to be really upset with you, but for different reasons. And when we found the first clue, we knew we were on the right track."

I held out the broken red and yellow "ASK ME" pin I had found in the dining room.

Uncle Joe looked puzzled and wondered who could possibly be upset with him.

"Me, for one!" Mr. Grady said. "I've been working here without a raise for years. The least you could've done is given me a few more dollars!"

Uncle Joe nodded. "Yeah, I guess you're right," he agreed. "Who else?"

"Chris Canarsie, who really wanted to become head chef," I said.

"But he doesn't know how to cook," Uncle Joe said. "I offered to send him to take classes somewhere, but he refused."

Daphne also pointed out that Mindy, the counselors at the lakefront, and the camp nurse also had some reasons to be upset. And then Fred mentioned Harriet Boyle.

"Not the tent thing," Uncle Joe said.

Harriet sat there in stony silence while

Entry #9

Daphne began to explain how the first clue we found — the red and yellow "ASK ME" pin — narrowed our suspect list down to three people. She added that we had to wait to find another clue before we could really start to get a handle on things.

"And that's where this key comes in," I said, holding up the key with the unusual engraving on it. Mr. Grady peered over my shoulder for a peek.

"Oh, the boathouse key," he said. "See there, I engraved a canoe inside a little house."

"And who would have a key to the boathouse?" asked Fred.

"Well, Harriet, of course," Uncle Joe reasoned. "And I guess Mr. Grady too."

"But not Chris Canarsie," I pointed out.

Uncle Joe nodded as the pieces started coming together in his mind.

"But it wasn't until we found the last clue behind the arts and crafts shack that we knew for certain it was Harriet," Fred said.

Mindy's eyes lit up. "Oh!" she exclaimed. "The purple lanyard!"

Daphne and I nodded in unison.

"I helped them with that one!" Mindy continued. "I told them that I hadn't received my shipment of lanyard strings yet, so it must've belonged to someone who already had one."

"And it matched the lanyard we saw Harriet carrying when we first met her," I summed up.

"And once we knew it was her, I was able to get help from Mr. Grady," Fred said.

"But why go through all this trouble, Harriet?" asked Uncle Joe.

"Because I wanted to get back at you for making me sleep in that stupid tent all summer long," she sneered. "I figured that since you ruined my summer, I was going to ruin your summer. And it was all going along swimmingly until that meddling old camper of yours and his friends showed up with their pestering pooch!"

Uncle Joe shook his head sympathetically.

"I'm sorry, Harriet, but it's part of the new health and safety codes I'm required to follow," Uncle Joe explained. "Every waterfront director —"

"Lakefront," Harriet said.

"Sorry. Every lakefront director has to reside within fifty yards of the lake," Uncle Joe said. "But there's nothing in the rules that says it has to be in a tent. Maybe Mr. Grady can fix up the back of the boathouse for you or something."

Mr. Grady's right eye squinted shut and he looked off into the distance.

"I can probably work something out," he nodded. "For a small raise, that is."

Uncle Joe smiled. "Done, and done!" he declared. "Boy, if I can run this camp just half as well as you kids solve mysteries, we should be in for a great summer. I don't know how to thank you."

"Like, how about letting us finish lunch?" Shaggy asked.

"I've got a better idea," Uncle Joe said. And he invited us to stay on as the guests of honor at the big pre-camp cookout that night.

"Sounds great!" Fred said.

"As for the rest of you, let's get this place cleaned up," Uncle Joe said. "Tomorrow's a big day for us. It's the first day of Camp Sakasnaks!"

The counselors cheered as Shaggy whispered to Scooby, "Like, one day, Scoob, maybe you can have your own camp," Shaggy said. "And we'll call it, Camp Scoobysnaks!" Shaggy said.

Scooby wagged his tail.

"Scooby-Dooby-Doo!" he sang.

Congratulations . . . you did it! We think you've got what it takes to be an honorary member of Mystery, Inc! So be on the lookout for more Scooby-Doo Case Files! We'll be glad to have you come along and help solve another mystery with me, Fred, Daphne, Shaggy, and of course, Scooby-Doo!